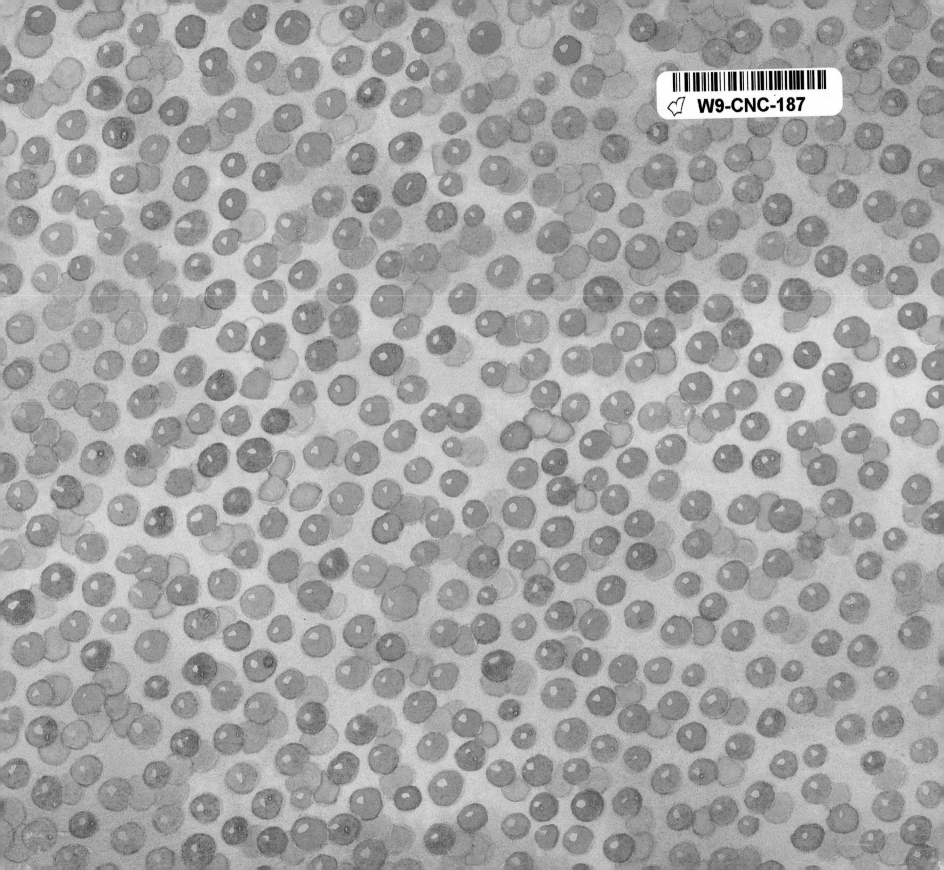

To my dad and his "Bangy" peas -S.S.

To David, my King Full of Beans -J.D.

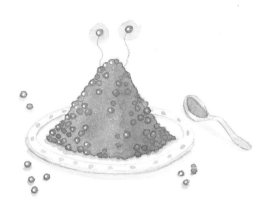

tiger tales

an imprint of ME Media, LLC

202 Old Ridgefield Road, Wilton, CT 06897

Published in the United States 2008

Originally published in Great Britain 2008

by Little Tiger Press

an imprint of Magi Publications

Text copyright © 2008 Steve Smallman

Illustrations copyright © 2008 Joelle Dreidemy

CIP data is available

ISBN-13: 978-1-58925-076-5

ISBN-10: 1-58925-076-1

Printed in Singapore

Smelly Peter
The Great Pea Eater

by **Steve Smallman**

Illustrated by
Joelle Dreidemy

tiger tales

Young Peter Pod was a little bit odd.
He ate nothing but peas, fresh or canned.
For breakfast and brunch, for dinner and lunch
'til he tooted just like a brass band!

Then early one morning,
without any warning,
Peter turned green as a pea.

I Love Peas

pOop

toot

He thought he looked cool, and he rushed off to school, so that all of his classmates could see.

But some kids like to tease
boys the color of peas.
They were nasty
to Peter all day.

At the back of the class,
in a cloud of green gas,
Peter thought about
running away.

That night, after dark, Peter ran to the park.

The stars were all twinkly and bright.

He saw a strange glow, then a big UFO

came and whisked him off into the night.

Some little green men stared at Peter and then, they knelt down and started to sing,
"You're the loveliest **green** that we've ever seen.
Oh, please say you'll be our new **king!**"

Peter agreed, so they shot off at speed
to the planet of Krell far away.

Then they asked if King Pete would like something to eat and he said,
"I'll have **peas**, if I may."

"What's a **pea?**"
asked the cooks
and exchanged worried looks,
for they'd made him a Krellian pie,
plus a wonderful feast, so that Peter at least
had to give half the dishes a try.

The food was all right! Peter squeaked with delight!
Then they all had a marvelous party.
And the funny thing was, they all loved him because
he was green and incredibly farty!

For a while, things went well
for the new king of Krell,
but then Peter began to feel sad.
Though the planet was ace
and he liked outer space,
he was missing his mom, dog, and dad.

Then Peter turned **PINK**—
(**lack** of peas do you think?)—
which upset all the people of Krell.
They'd wanted a lean, green farting machine,
and now he'd stopped farting as well.

They took off his crown
and his velvety gown.
There were angry green
faces all 'round him.

Boot!

Then without a farewell,
the ex-king of Krell
was dumped back on the earth
where they'd found him.

"Hey, look it's our Peter!
He's pink and smells sweeter.
And he's hungry.
We know what that means...."

But Peter said, "Please!
Don't give me those peas!
From now on I just want...